NO LONGER
PROPERTY OF PPLD

NO LONGER
PROPERTY OF PPLD

D1505783

JEASY
ORGI

PIKES PEAK LIBRARY DISTRICT
COLORADO SPRINGS CO 80901-1579
Go-go baby!

156745135

For Charlotte,
the original Go-Go Baby
—R. O.

To Pat Lindgren and
Piper Smith, for all your
care and expertise
throughout the years
—S. S.

Go-Go Baby!

by **Roxane Orgill**   illustrations by **Steven Salerno**

MARSHALL CAVENDISH   NEW YORK   LONDON   SINGAPORE

Naptime—
no!

**Sleepytime—
not *my* sister.**

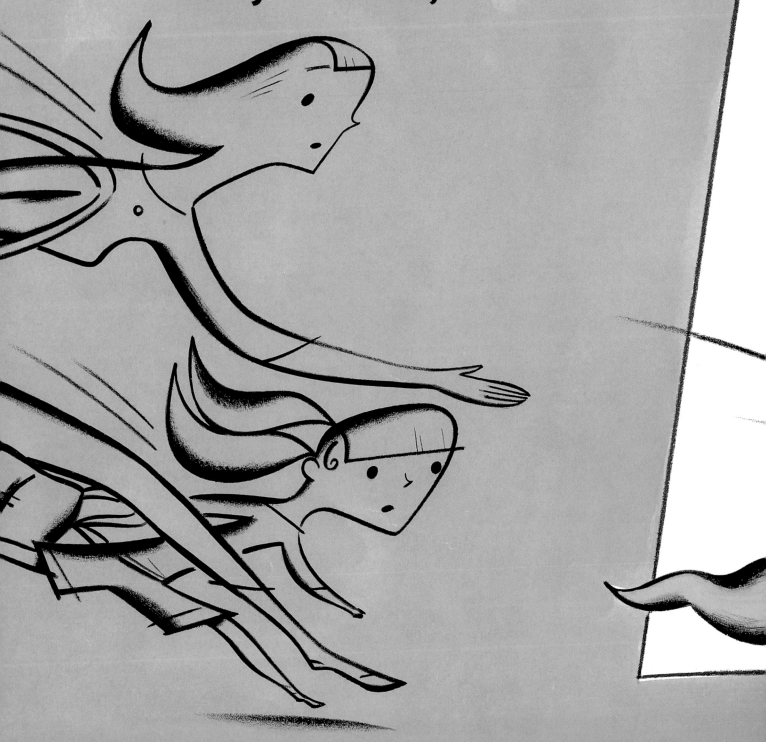

**She's Go-Go Baby
ready to ramble,**

buckle up,

ROLL...

Naptime—

not so fast!
Go-Go Baby's

on a stroll . . .

To the bus!

Doors hiss,
open close,
jingle-jangle coins.

Va-*rooom* goes the motor.
Love that roar.

Love to go!

**Naptime—
not now!**

**Go-Go Baby's
moving on . . .**

To the train!

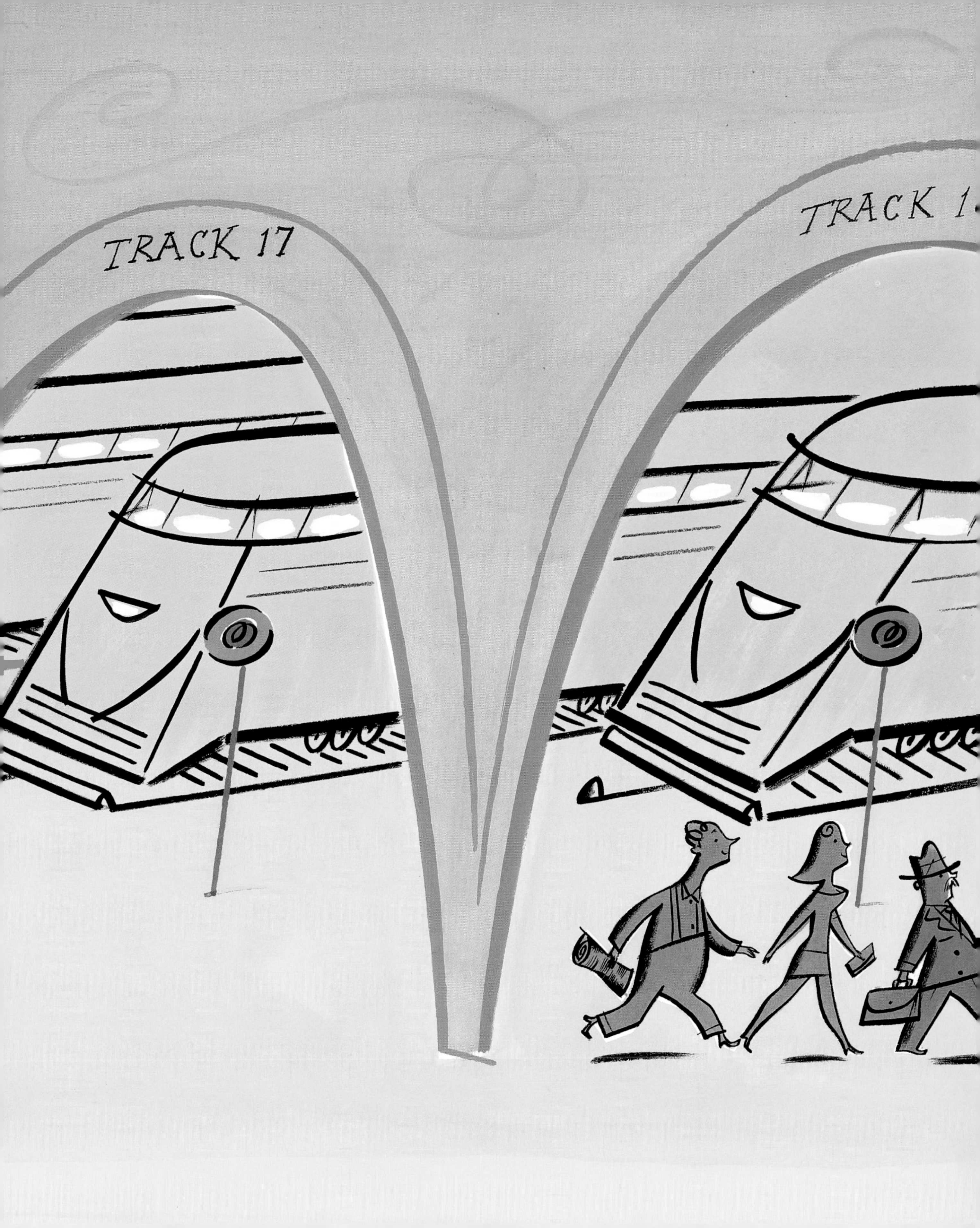
TRACK 17
TRACK

Punch punch.
"Tickets please!"
Wheels clicky clack.

Woo-*ooo* goes the whistle.
Love that noise.

Love to go!

**Naptime—
not yet!
Go-Go Baby's
still on a roll . . .**

Uh-oh!

Ramp!

To the ferry!

**Dock squeaks,
water slaps,
snapping windy flag.**

Ba-*ronk* goes the horn.
Love that racket.

Love to go!

**Sleepytime—
soon!**

**Go-Go Baby's
rolling on**

and on . . .

sleepy baby

going . . .

going . . .

Gone!

Text copyright © 2004 by Roxane Orgill
Illustrations copyright © 2004 by Steven Salerno
All rights reserved
Marshall Cavendish, 99 White Plains Road, Tarrytown, NY 10591
www.marshallcavendish.com
Library of Congress Cataloging-in-Publication Data

Orgill, Roxane.
Go-go baby! / by Roxane Orgill ; illustrations by Steven Salerno.—
1st ed.
p. cm.
"Marshall Cavendish."
Summary: A mother and her five-year-old take the energetic baby on an
outing and end up chasing a runaway stroller.
ISBN 0-7614-5157-9
[1. Babies—Fiction. 2. Brothers and sisters—Fiction.] I. Salerno,
Steven, ill. II. Title.
PZ7.O6325Go 2004
[E]—dc21
2003009320

The text of this book is set in Meta.
The illustrations are rendered in gouache.
Book design by Sonar Gonzales

Printed in China
First edition
1 3 5 6 4 2